W9-BQX-384

Dear Parents,

Welcome to the Scholastic Reader series. We have taken over 80 years of experience with teachers, parents, and children and put it into a program that is designed to match your child's interests and skills.

Level 1—Short sentences and stories made up of words kids can sound out using their phonics skills and words that are important to remember.

Level 2—Longer sentences and stories with words kids need to know and new "big" words that they will want to know.

Level 3—From sentences to paragraphs to longer stories, these books have large "chunks" of texts and are made up of a rich vocabulary.

Level 4—First chapter books with more words and fewer pictures.

It is important that children learn to read well enough to succeed in school and beyond. Here are ideas for reading this book with your child:

- Look at the book together. Encourage your child to read the title and make a prediction about the story.
- Read the book together. Encourage your child to sound out words when appropriate. When your child struggles, you can help by providing the word.
- Encourage your child to retell the story. This is a great way to check for comprehension.
- Have your child take the fluency test on the last page to check progress.

Scholastic Readers are designed to support your child's efforts to learn how to read at every age and every stage. Enjoy helping your child learn to read and love to read.

   —Francie Alexander
   Chief Education Officer
   Scholastic Education

To Alice, Jean, Joanne, and lunch
—M.S.

For Samantha and Stephanie,
my two treasures
—J.S.

No part of this publication may be reproduced in whole or in part,
or stored in a retrieval system, or transmitted in any form or by any means,
electronic, mechanical, photocopying, recording, or otherwise, without written permission
of the publisher. For information regarding permission, write to Scholastic Inc.,
Attention: Permissions Department, 557 Broadway, New York, NY 10012.

Text copyright © 2001 by Mary Serfozo.
Illustrations copyright © 2001 by Jeffrey Scherer.
Fluency activities copyright © 2003 Scholastic Inc.

All rights reserved. Published by Scholastic Inc.
SCHOLASTIC, CARTWHEEL BOOKS, and associated logos are trademarks
and/or registered trademarks of Scholastic Inc.

Library of Congress Cataloging-in-Publication Data is available.

ISBN 0-439-59426-X

10 9 8 7 6 5 4 3 2   07 08 09 10
Printed in the U.S.A.   23
First printing, April 2001

THE BIG BUG DUG

by Mary Serfozo
Illustrated by Jeffrey Scherer

Scholastic Reader — Level 1

Cartwheel
·B·O·O·K·S· ®

SCHOLASTIC INC.
New York Toronto London Auckland Sydney
Mexico City New Delhi Hong Kong Buenos Aires

The big bug dug

. . . and dug

. . . and dug.

Down in the dirt,
the big bug dug.

Dug past a snake.

Dug past
a slug.

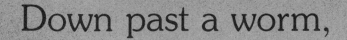

Down past a worm,

the big bug dug.

Down past

the roots

and gopher holes.

Down past the rocks.

Down past the moles.

And still on down,
down from the top,
the big bug dug.

Where would he stop?

He didn't stop
for lunch or nap.

He didn't stop
to check the map.

Just dug on down,
that big old bug.

And dug and dug
and dug and dug.

Until he met . . .

no one at all.

No moles, no gophers
came to call.

No worms, no slugs,
no sounds to hear.

Then the big bug said,
"At last—I'm here!

"No bug should have
to dig so deep
to find a quiet
place to sleep!"

ZZZZZZZzzzzzz

Opposites

Opposite words mean something completely different from each other. For example, **high** is the opposite of **low**. Draw a line to match each word with its opposite.

top	**little**
down	**go**
big	**bottom**
stop	**up**

Surprise! Surprise!

Connect the dots from A to Z for a surprise.

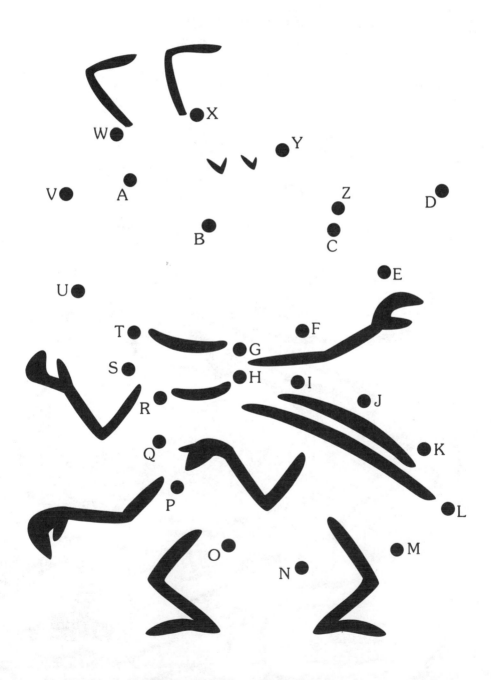

A-maze-ing Bug

Help the big bug find
a quiet place to sleep.

START

FINISH

A Rhyme for You

Fun and **sun** are words that rhyme. In each row, circle the picture that rhymes with the word.

dug

rocks

map

hear

call

A Buggy Word Find

The word BUG is hidden in this word find
puzzle ten times. Look up, down, and across.
See if you can find them all.

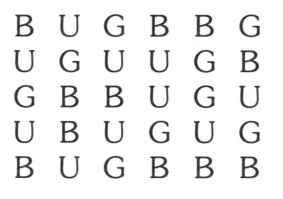

B U G B B G
U G U U G B
G B B U G U
U B U G U G
B U G B B B

Fill in the Blanks

Where did the big bug dig?

He dug down in the **d__rt**.

What did the big bug pass?

He dug past a **w__r__**.

What was the big bug looking for?

He was looking for a quiet place

to **s__e__p**.

ANSWERS

Opposites

top
little

down
go

big
bottom

stop
up

Surprise! Surprise!

A-maze-ing Bug

A Rhyme for You

dug

rocks

map

hear

call

Fill in the Blanks

He dug down in the d**i**rt.

He dug past a w**or**m.

He was looking for a quiet place to s**lee**p.

A Buggy Word Find

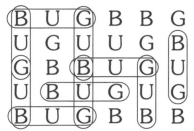